Dachy's
Deaf

Written and illustrated by Jack Hughes

WINDMILL
BOOKS ™

New York

Published in 2015 by Windmill Books, An Imprint of Rosen Publishing
29 East 21st Street, New York, NY 10010

Text and illustrations © Jack Hughes 2012

US Editor: Joshua Shadowens
Editor: Victoria Brooker
Design: Lisa Peacock and Steve Prosser

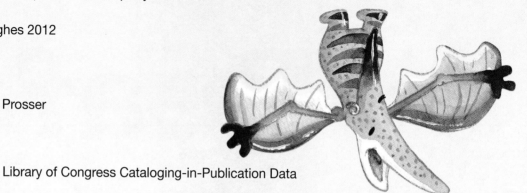

Library of Congress Cataloging-in-Publication Data

Hughes, Jack, author, illustrator.
 Dachy's deaf / by Jack Hughes.
    pages cm. — (Dinosaur friends)
 Summary: "Dachy wears a hearing aid. But sometimes, when his friends get too noisy, he likes to
turn it off to get some peace and quiet. One day, when his hearing aid is off, Dachy falls asleep and ends
up floating down the river towards a waterfall and a hungry crocodile. Can his friends rescue him in time?
— Provided by publisher.
 Includes index.
 ISBN 978-1-4777-9222-3 (library binding) — ISBN 978-1-4777-9223-0 (pbk.) —
 ISBN 978-1-4777-9224-7 (6-pack)
 [1. Deaf—Fiction. 2. Hearing aids—Fiction. 3. People with disabilities—Fiction. 4. Friendship—Fiction.
5. Dinosaurs—Fiction.] I. Title.
 PZ7.H87329Dac 2015
 [E]—dc23
                            2013048837

Manufactured in the United States of America

CPSIA Compliance Information: Batch #WS14WM: For Further Information contact Windmill Books, New York, New York at 1-866-478-0556

Contents

BUZZZZZZZZZ!

Dachy wore a hearing aid. With his hearing aid, Dachy could hear many sounds. BUZZZZZZZZZZ! The gentle buzzing sound of a busy bumblebee.

4

TWEET, TWEET, TWEET! The sound of a bird singing high above. SWISH, SWISH, SWISH! The sound the wind makes as it gently blows through the trees.

TWEET! TWEET! TWEET!

However, when Dachy's hearing aid was switched off, he could hear very little at all.

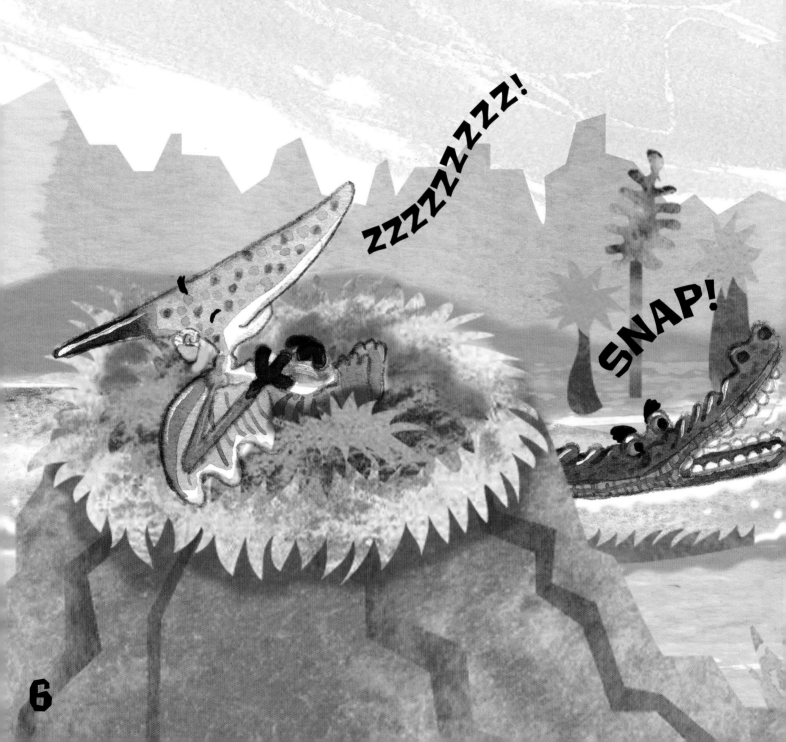

7

Sometimes Dachy's friends were far too noisy. They would BANG! They would CRASH! They would SHOUT! until Dachy could hear nothing but NOISE!

HA HA!

HO HO!

HEE! HEE!

8

One day, Dachy's friends were being particularly
noisy. Emmy and Steggie were laughing loudly,
and Rex kept shouting too close to Dachy's ears.

Not wanting to spoil their fun, Dachy flew off for a rest. He turned off his hearing aid and sat down on a rock for a rest and some peace and quiet.

But it wasn't a rock! It was a very large, rather grumpy, Turtle. "Get off!" grumbled the Turtle rudely. But Dachy couldn't hear him. "I said, GET OFF!" the Turtle shouted angrily.

13

Dachy did not hear the Turtle. He did not move.
Dachy had fallen asleep! He then began to snore
very loudly! The grumpy Turtle was very angry.
14 He wandered off towards the river to get a drink.

15

As the grumpy Turtle knelt to drink the water, Dachy slid off his shell and landed on a passing log. Still fast asleep, Dachy began to float slowly downstream.

17

Rex, Emmy and Steggie noticed Dachy had disappeared and were looking for him. They had reached the riverbank when Emmy suddenly spotted Dachy. "Oh my goodness, look!" she cried.

Dachy was heading for a waterfall...
and at the bottom of the waterfall
was a very hungry looking alligator.

19

"DACHY, WAKE UP!" they all shouted. "Oh no!" cried Rex, realizing that Dachy couldn't hear them. Rex had a plan. "Come on, everyone. Follow me!" he called, and ran off as fast as he could.

21

They stopped at the edge of the riverbank, a little
bit ahead of Dachy. Rex grabbed a tree branch
and clambered onto Emmy's long neck. Emmy
stretched out as far as she could across the water.
With the long stick, Rex prodded Dachy awake.

23

Dachy jolted up and flew into the air just before the log tumbled over the waterfall and into the mouth of the alligator.

Aargh, ALLIGATOR!!

25

Dachy landed on the riverbank and turned his hearing aid
back on. "Oh my goodness, how did I get here!" he said.
"We're not exactly sure," Rex replied. "Why did you turn off
your hearing aid, Dachy?" asked Emmy with concern.

27

"Well I don't like it when you all shout. I can't hear what anyone is saying," explained Dachy. "Oh, Dachy, we're so sorry," they all agreed. "We promise not to be so noisy next time we're playing."

"And I promise to let someone know where I'm going if I want to be on my own next time," said Dachy.

As the friends headed back into the forest they all listened quietly to the wonderful sounds all around them. What sounds do you think they could hear in the forest?

Glossary

alligator (A-luh-gay-ter) A large reptile with thick, rough skin and strong jaws.
bumblebee (BUM-bull-bee) A large bee with a thick, hairy body, usually banded with gold.
downstream (DOWN-streem) In the direction of the current of a stream.
hearing aid (HEER-ing AYD) A small instrument that fits on your ear. It makes sounds louder so they can be heard.
river (RIH-ver) A large natural stream of water that flows into a lake, ocean, or the like.
waterfall (WAH-ter-fol) A stream of water that falls from a high place.

Index

Further Reading

Beaumont, Steve. *Drawing Pteranodon and Other Flying Dinosaurs.* Drawing Dinosaurs. New York: PowerKids Press, 2010.

Royston, Angela. *Sound and Hearing.* Science Corner. New York: PowerKids Press, 2011.

Websites

For web resources related to the subject of this book, go to: www.windmillbooks.com/weblinks and select this book's title.